This book is dedicated to Sir David Attenborough and everyone doing their part to protect our planet.

Published by R & N Publishing.
Text Copyright © 2021, Reece May.
Illustrations © 2021, Alexandra Ball.

Printed in the UK. All materials are sourced from sustainably managed forests and the inks used are vegetable based.

ISBN: 978 1 83842 200 4

Annie the armadillo

Reece May and **Alexandra Ball**

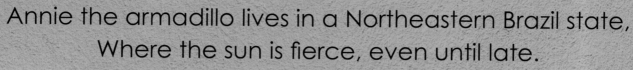

Annie the armadillo lives in a Northeastern Brazil state,
Where the sun is fierce, even until late.

She lives in a burrow which is underground,
Not far from her food in the termite mound!

In the cool of the burrow, she lives with Mum and Dad,
Along with her sister Faye we must add.

They all rest inside when it gets too hot,
The sisters think of games to play, so they plot.

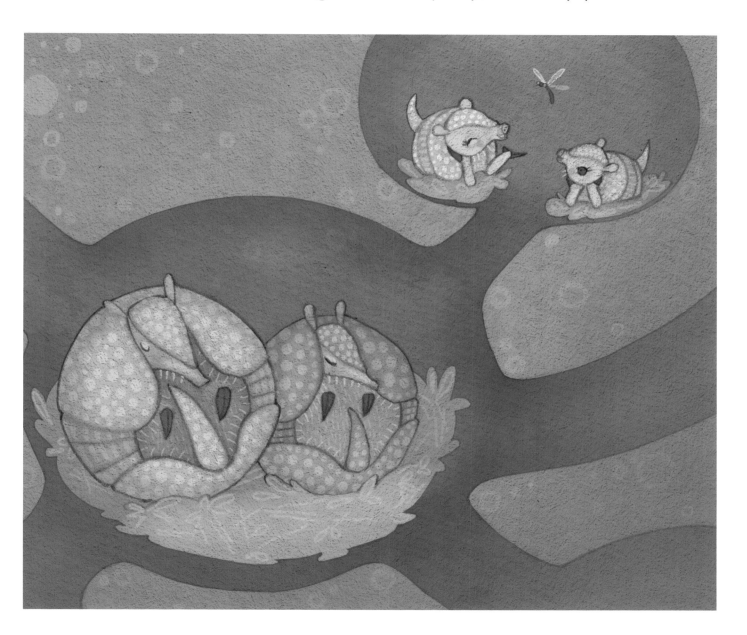

"Mrs Armadillo, you have such beautiful armour"
"Oh Mr Armadillo, you are such a charmer!"

"This kind of talk makes me feel sick!"
"I really hope it begins to cool down quick."

Looking out of the burrow, Dad sees the sun has set,
"Right girls, what do we do if there is a threat?"

"We do not fight, we don't stand tall,
Instead we roll up into a ball."

Digging into the mounds with their claws.
They eat the termites, without a second to pause.

Everyone has eaten as much as they can,
Now it's time for Annie and Faye to complete their plan.

"Mum, Dad, we are going to play"
"Okay girls, but in our sight, please stay!"

"Come on Faye let's climb this big termite hill,
Then we can race and I will win with my skill."

They climbed up the hill, to the very top,
"*Last one down, smells like cow plop!*"

Annie and Faye rolled down in a ball,

They zoomed and with great speed they did fall.

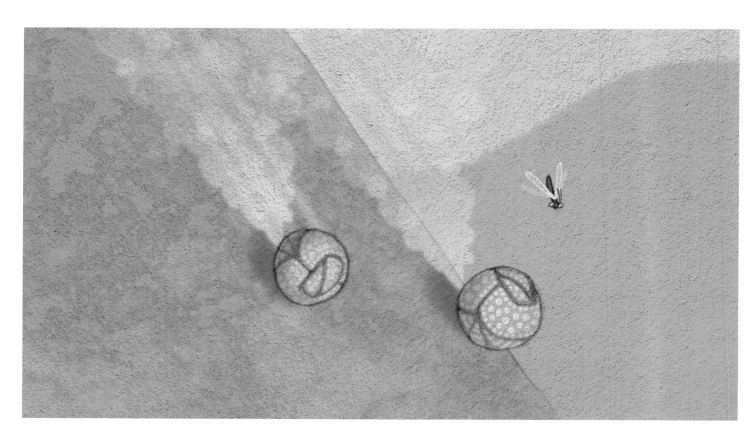

Not wanting to slow, they rolled out of sight,
But then when they stopped they were in for a **fright!**

Up in the clouds, an eagle looked down,
What were once smiles turned into a frown.

"*Mum, Dad!*" the sisters screamed,
The eagle dived as its eyes gleamed.

"Quick little sister, we cannot stand tall,
We must roll into our protective ball!"

The eagle came down and tried to lift Faye.
She was wrapped tightly, he couldn't take her away.
Then out of nowhere came a growing rumble,
It was Dad rolling down with an almighty tumble.

Dad rolled into the eagle with a big WHACK,
The eagle squawked and gave up on the attack.

"Quick children, back to the burrow!"
The sisters ran as fast as they could follow.

"My babies, I'm so glad you're okay!"
"Dad was amazing, he drove the eagle away."

"We got lucky this time, that's why you must stay...
In sight of your parents, whilst you play!"

Fun Facts: Armadillos

There are **21 species** of armadillo, but only two kinds can actually roll into a ball, like Annie. When they roll into a ball their boney plates on their back overlap.

Armadillos can be **brown**, **pink**, **black**, **grey**, **red** or **yellow**.

Size - Armadillos can be between **12.5cm** to **150cm** long.

Age - They usually live to be between **7-20 years** old!

Some armadillos can run at **30mph** and are **good swimmers**, holding their breath for up to **6 minutes**.